Mother Steals a Bicycle
and other stories

Salai Selvam and Shruti Buddhavarapu
Illustrations by Tejubehan

YOU CAN N-E-V-E-R TELL when my mother will break into a story. I secretly think she's always on the lookout for an opportunity to share one, especially with me. Amma tells me that when I was a baby and too little to understand anything, I would just listen to the way her voice went high and low as she told me story after story. She still does it, s l o w i n g d o w n her words to build suspense, or making them go faster and faster for stories in which she is running (or cycling) away from some kind of mischief.

I don't know if that baby story is true because I don't remember too much from that time. But I'm eleven-and-a-half now, and Amma's stories are kind of great. I would never tell her this, but they are better than any of the twenty-seven fantasy books in my school library—and I should know, I've read them all. The other day, while fussing over my scraped knee with some ointment, she told me about how she and her friends would crush the leaves of plants to apply on their bruises, and how it would magically heal them. "But how did you know which ones to pick?" I asked. "We just did," Amma replied. I want to know how to do that too.

Almost all of Amma's stories as a child are from her village.
Listening to her adventures there as a kid always makes me want
to go there again and again. It would be so great if I could have
these adventures! My school and friends are okay, and sometimes
fun, but they are nothing like Amma's.

Sometimes, when we sleep on the terrace together when it's too
hot, Amma tells me a story and falls asleep in the middle of it.
But then I look at the stars up in the sky and squint and pretend
they are the twinkling eyes of wild animals in Amma's stories.
And sometimes, if Amma starts snor-r-r-ing—a little,
not a lot—I can't help but think of grasshoppers and giggle.

But is there a place where hyenas and baby peacocks wander
around humans? Where children like me are allowed to walk
to school alone and have feasts with their friends under the
moonlight? Did Amma really steal a bicycle, and is it even
possible to wrestle your shadow?

I'm not sure. But I'll share a few of my favourite tales,
and maybe you can decide.

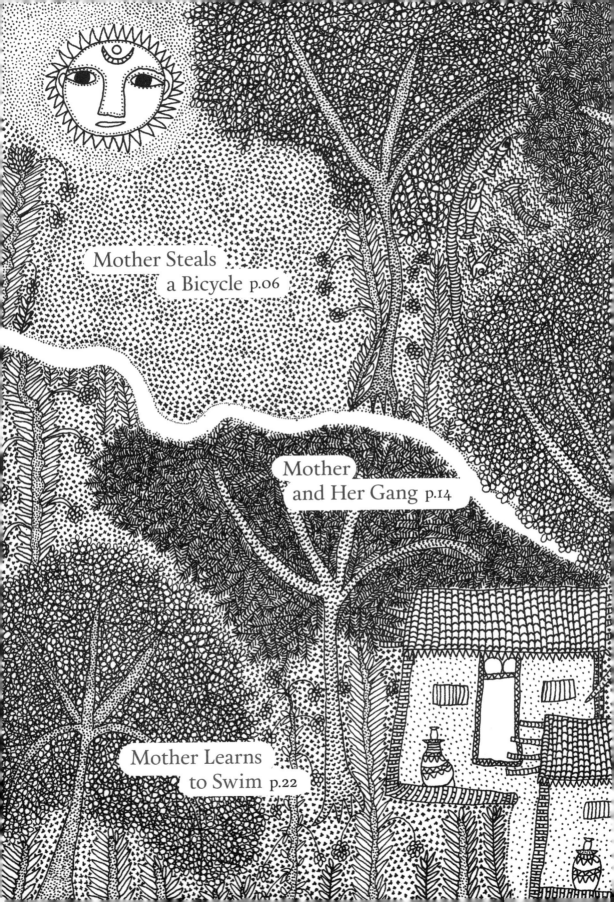

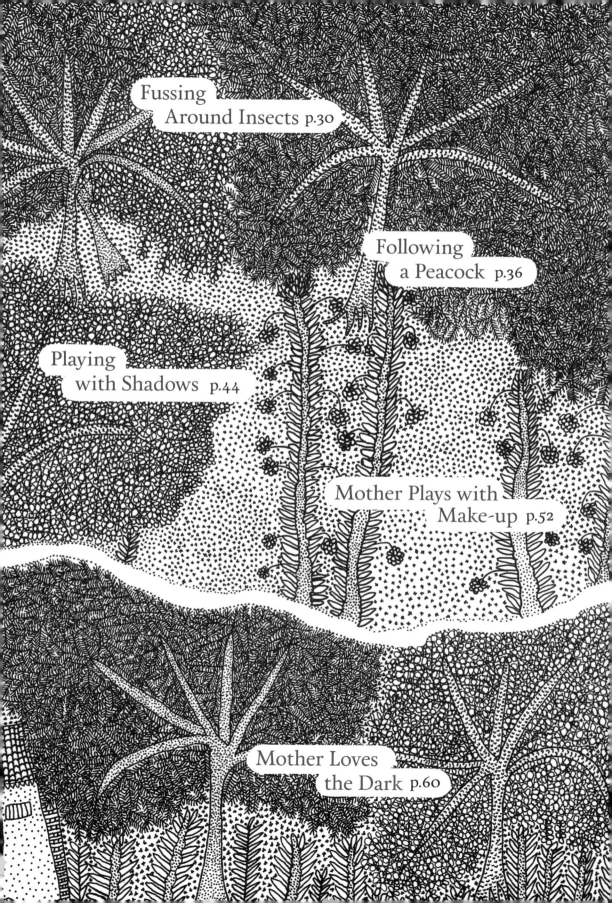

AMMA'S BEST STORIES are ones where trouble actually comes looking for her. This one with the cycle might top them all.

Someone had come visiting Amma's house, on a cycle. This was a special moment, because not a lot of people owned cycles at the time, so seeing one was rare.

"I just wanted to ride one so badly," Amma told me.

"Did you borrow his cycle while he was there, to learn?"

"No... I figured that the visitor would stay for a while, so I sneaked out and quietly wheeled the bike away from home," she replied, sheepishly.

"You stole the cycle!" I said, astonished.

"Just borrowed it for a few hours," Amma said with a wink.

"But you said you didn't even know how to ride a cycle..."

"No, but it had looked pretty easy when I saw other people doing it. You just had to sit and pedal, pedal, pedal. Easy! So I lugged the cycle onto the main road and told myself the time had come to ride it. But there was one small problem..."

"What?"

"The cycle was taller than me, so I needed help getting onto the seat."

"Ha! So, then?"

"Then I looked around for a bit, hoping for a passerby who could help prop me up on the seat. A few minutes later, I spotted someone and called out, 'Uncle! Can you please hold my bike so I can get on it?'"

"What did he say?"

"He seemed willing, holding on until I started pedalling.

Once I saw that my feet reached the pedals comfortably, I asked him to let go, and started pedalling away."

"And you didn't fall off?"

"No, I somehow had it going, and monkey-pedalled down the road, away from the fellow who helped me. I heard him shouting, 'My God! I really hope you know how to cycle!'"

"And that's how you learnt how to cycle?"

"I wouldn't really call it 'cycling'. Let's just say that the cycle was moving along on its own, and very fast. I just kept my feet on the pedals and grabbed the handlebars hard. I veered off the main roads and went down paths that I knew from walking. I zoomed past one village, then another, and then another. At one point, I wanted to stop and take a small break but realised that I didn't actually know how to stop riding the cycle. So I had to do what I did earlier..."

"Ask someone else to stop you?"

"Yes."

"You could have just used your brakes, Amma."

"Yes, but you must remember that this was the first time I was on a cycle."

"Oh, yes. So did your plan work? Did you finally stop?"

"Well I was going so fast that when I finally did see some people about, I whizzed past them before I could even open my mouth!"

"Did you try waving your hands or yelling out loudly for help?"

"Yes, but I was afraid that doing anything would throw me off balance and I'd crash, along with this cycle that I'd borrowed. So I decided to do the only thing I could do... continue cycling. I couldn't keep it up, of course, I was so tired. I even thought for a second that if I jumped off the path, the cycle would just stop on its own."

"That's so silly!"

"Back then I really thought that the cycle was only meant for paths, and that if there were no paths, the cycle would automatically stop working."

I burst out laughing, surprised at young Amma's logic.

"Did that work?"

"Sort of. I tried directing the cycle

off the path, and before I knew it, I had fallen into a dry water canal. I was flat on the ground, with the cycle on me, one wheel spinning away. I tried clambering up but it hurt all over."

"Ow!" I winced.

"So I just lay back for a moment and looked up at the sky…"

"You took a nap after the accident?" I asked, confused.

"No, I just lay there for a bit. I had to get home. Even if everything was hurting. I had to pick myself up and carry the cycle out of the canal."

"Did you cry Amma?"

"I did, a little. Actually, I really just wanted someone to come pick me up, dust my clothes and carry me back home. But I was all alone. So I used all my strength to push the cycle off me and

managed to stand up slowly. I looked at my hands—they were all scratched and bleeding. And then I think I started crying, because it was scary."

"So how did you get out of the canal?"

"I saw a trail from the canal that linked up to the main path. So I pushed the cycle—which was now so heavy—slowly up that trail."

"How can a cycle put on weight? I'm sure it was heavy in the morning too."

"Yes, but then the cycle was carrying me. I was so tired and it hurt so much that I decided to scream."

"What! Really?"

"Yes! I started with a low eEEEEEEEeeeeeee and then followed it with **OoOoOoOoOoOoo**."

"Haha! Did that work?"

"I felt a lot better. I also kept count of the tamarind trees that I passed on my way. They seemed to go on and on. Then, I saw a huge *elanthai* tree full of fruit. I had a big decision to make."

"What was it?" I asked impatiently. Did she spot a hyena? Did she have to throw the cycle into a ditch and run home? Was she going to spend the night in the canal?

"To eat fruit, or not to eat fruit?"

"**Ammaaaaaaaaaa!**"

"I had to distract myself from the pain! Anyway, I decided not to eat the fruit because I had to get home. Plus by this time I was also starting to feel a little guilty about having done something wrong. I just wanted it all to be over, so I kept going with the cycle."

"You walked all the way back home?" I asked astonished.

"I had to. Although, after walking what I thought had to be around fifty kilometres, something happened. I heard a rumbling sound— it was a motorbike! The only person who owned one in these parts was from my village, so I was relieved."

"Did you call for help?"

"No…before I could do anything, the sound disappeared. He'd obviously taken another way. So I walked some more and started thinking of what to do when it got dark. Maybe I'd have to sleep under a tree. I was so lost in my thoughts that I didn't notice I had stumbled into a village I knew—it wasn't too far from home."

"Did you at least ask for help now?"

"Oh I was ready to scream:
'HELP! HELP! I fell off my bike and have been walking for miles carrying it. HELP! HELP! I am hurt and tired from walking this bike!'…but the words wouldn't come out."

"Why?"

"I was thinking of how happily I had sailed along in the morning; how the bike had sped past trees and ponds and huts and how I had wanted to go on and on, where I was sure I'd find the sea. If only I hadn't thought of how to stop cycling! I'd still be on my way to the seashore…"

Amma paused for a second before continuing.

"Anyway, I decided that I'd rather walk home by myself and put off the scolding for a bit. Plus, that would give me enough time to come up with a story I could tell my mother and the visitor about what happened with the cycle. Would I find him outside my house, searching frantically for his cycle, I wondered…"

Amma didn't say. I'd liked to have known.

Mother
and Her Gang

IN MOST OF HER STORIES, Amma seems fearless. Things that make me shudder seem to excite her and it makes me wonder how we are related. If you think of it, nearly every adventure she had was because she wasn't scared. But I find it hard to believe that she was never scared, and so I asked her once about it.

"What were you most scared of as a child, Amma?"

She took a moment to think.

"Hmm. Maybe all those long distances we walked to school? There were some scary moments in that walk," she said.

"How long was it?"

"Let's see…we must have walked nearly five kilometres to and from school every day. That's from Class 1 to Class 8. I never went alone, though. But even though my friends and I always walked in a group, we would feel a bit scared, especially walking through dense forest paths."

"How were you allowed to walk by yourselves?" I asked.

"Well, usually a teacher had to accompany us. But a few of us liked slipping away by ourselves," she explained.

"So…you weren't scared then?" I asked, trying to understand how this related to my question.

"See, there were two paths we could take to school: a long, straight road and a shortcut. We were all supposed to use only the straight road, since it was paved. It even had a huge sign:

'ATTENTION! USE ONLY THIS ROAD FOR WALKING'.

But no one paid any attention to it. Why walk more when you can use a shorter path? So those who walked to school would use the shortcut and those who went by bullock cart or cycle took the straight road," she explained.

"So you took the shortcut?"

"Well… yes and no. The problem was that the shortcut took us too quickly to school… so we wandered around a bit, making our own paths."

"Who did you go with?"

"I had a small gang of friends. Our parents didn't own bullock carts and we didn't have cycles, so we walked. Soon knew all the paths to school and chose a different one each day. We named each path: I remember a peanut-field-path, a pond-path, a temple-path, a snake-path…"

"A whole field of peanuts!" I exclaimed.

"Once we saw a monkey grab a peanut stalk from the field and tie it around its stomach like a belt. That looked like so much fun that we just had to copy it! In all that tying and laughing, we were late for school. But you know, we were all also so easily distracted—all kinds of little things made us stop."

"Really? Like what?"

"Like, we'd suddenly spot a snake and stop in our tracks, terrified. Or one of us would spot a chameleon in a bush and the rest of the gang would gather around it—waiting to see its next move. And if it was a tree full of fruit, there was only one thing to do: sit under the tree, and stuff ourselves with fruit!"

"But weren't you on your way to school…?"

"Oh, we didn't care…until we saw the school, that is. And then we would make a run for it, hoping to slip into our classroom just before the school bell rang. We were nearly always late, though. And then we would stand at the classroom door, panting and looking so sheepish that our teacher would have to relent. But, the second that the school bell rang at the end of the day, we would *bolt* out of the classrooms, eager to get home to play."

"You ran with your heavy school bags?" I asked.

"We found a way around it. We'd throw our bags as far ahead of us as we could and then race to pick them up. We were so busy racing each other and throwing our bags that we hardly noticed how heavy they were, or how long the route was."

Maybe we are related after all. I've often thought of throwing my bag too. And then run in the other direction.

"But didn't you ruin your school bags?" I asked.

"Well, we didn't do it all the time. Sometimes we'd get on a passing bullock cart and hang our bags on it. Not all cart-men let us on though, and if they yelled at us, we would jump off, leave our bags there and simply jog along with the cart...all the way home."

"It's unfair that all these amazing things happened only in your village!"

Amma let out a chuckle.

"I had a friend from the Andamans… Kanaka… she had so many more stories to tell. And her stories seemed more unbelievable than anything in our village."

"What did she say?"

"She claimed that the forest path in our village was nothing compared to the ones back in the Andamans…"

"Wait, the forest-path that you took on your shortcut to school? The one you all found scary?" I interrupted.

"Yes. She said you could still at least look up and see the blue sky on our village path. But according to her, the trees in the Andaman forests were so huge and grew so closely together that once you stepped inside the forest you couldn't even tell if it was day or night."

"Because the trees didn't let any light through?"

Amma nodded.

That did sound scary.

"Where is she now?" I asked.

"Hmm…I think she left after Class 8."

"She went back to the Andamans?"

"I don't really know."

"But she didn't tell you? I thought you were friends."

"I don't remember her telling us she was leaving. But by the time we were all in Class 8, we started hurrying to school on the straight road, and took the other paths less and less. And each time we took a different path, Kanaka would say: 'This is the last time I'm walking this path.' But if that was her way of telling us she was leaving, we certainly didn't catch on…"

I left Amma to her thoughts after that, but I realised later that she didn't really answer my question about being scared. Maybe another time…

Mother Learns
to Swim

I LOVE MY GEOGRAPHY CLASS. Especially when we learn about different water bodies because I just love water.

My teacher had pointed to India on a huge map hanging by the blackboard and said, "India is bordered by the Himalayas in the north, the Indian Ocean in the south, by the Bay of Bengal in the east and the Arabian Sea to its west."

I looked at the borders of India—it is surrounded by so much blue! I wish I could see all of it for real.

I ran home after school and told Amma about geography class and she said that she had the same lesson in school when she was my age.

"Did you like water too, Amma?" I asked her.

"Oh I loved it! I wanted to know what lay beyond India, and how I could get there. Was it just like walking from one village to the next, I wondered. Then all of us in class decided we wanted to make our own map."

"But there can only be one map for India, right?" I asked, puzzled.

"Oh, we wanted to make a map of our own village since we didn't have one. So we substituted local place names: 'Ooral Hills to the east; Kallodai Pond to the west; Koothini Canal to the south and Phukini Canal to the north!'"

"But how did you know, if there was no map for your village?"

"Our elders told us what surrounded our village. That's how we found out that there were hills on one side of the village, and water on the other. Actually, ours was the only village for miles that had so much water all around."

"Ooooh! Did you swim a lot? Were kids even allowed to swim in ponds?"

"Oh, I was always in the water. Any excuse to jump into a pond.

I was there at all times of the day, it didn't matter how hot
or cold it was. I knew everything about every pond, lake
and canal. I knew where I would find lots of fish, where the
water turned green with moss and where I could feel soft
sand below my feet."

Amma lay back in the chair.

"And it was not just me, our entire gang was crazy about water.
Other people used to hate when the ponds flooded during the
rainy season, but it would make us so happy. We were amazed
at how much water there was in the rainy months, and how
the ponds went as dry as deserts in April and May."

"That's because it is seasonal, just like the life cycles of animals,
right Amma?"

"Yes, well caught! Back then the rains almost always came
on time... not like it is now, where ponds are always dry.
And guess what we used to do when it rained a lot?"

"What?"

"We walked in the rain, deliberately stepping into every
puddle that came in our way. We loved the sound our feet made
when they hit the wet, muddy ground. splosh splosh splosh!"

"You never allow me to play in the rain!" I complained.

"Because there's a road outside our house, not a forest.
You need to be careful about cars and bikes, especially during
rainy season," Amma explained.

I nodded slowly.

"What other fun things did you do, Amma!"

"Mmm... let's see, sometimes, after it rained, we would take
a thin towel and float it in the pond to try and catch some fish.
Younger children would scoop up the muddy waters of the pond,

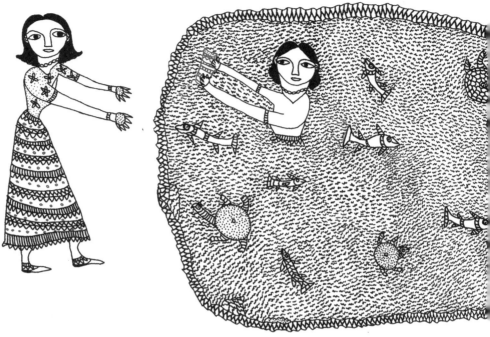

pour them into buckets
and hold out tumblers, yelling
'Coffeeeeeeeeee, coooooFFEEEEEEeeeeee!!
Who wants coffee?'"

"Haha! Did you buy any?"

"No, I was busy with more important things," Amma said
with a mischievous smile.

"Like?"

"Like learning how to swim!"

"Did you learn it all by yourself?"

"Somewhat. At first, I just followed the older children into the
water. I'd throw my arms about, trying to stay afloat. I'm sure
it looked very odd and funny. People even teased me about it.
I ended up swallowing a lot of water this way, but didn't give up
and came back to the pond day after day. I'd hold onto the washing
stone and thrash about in the water until I felt comfortable in it.

Then, I learned to $float$, and then to move through the water. Once I felt at home in it, I had a friend tie an inflated cycle tube to my waist and went as deep as I could in the pond."

"Why didn't you just ask a someone who knew swimming?"

"But where's the fun in that?" Amma asked, gently poking me in the arm.

Amma continued. "But this wasn't enough for me. I wanted to learn to swim in the big village well. It was smaller than the pond, but there you had to dive into the water. There was no other way."

"Diving! Isn't that dangerous?"

"Well… I had a dried bottle gourd tied to my back, an inflated cycle tube round my middle. An older girl who sat on the well's edge held one end of a sari. The other end was tied to my waist… I would be let down and dragged up and this was how I learned to dive."

"How long did it take you?"

"Maybe a year? My lessons didn't just end there though. After mastering the pond and well, swimming across a water canal was easy. We would then hold competitions—who could get first to the other side of the bank? Who can stay underwater for the longest?"

"That sounds like a lot more fun. All I get to swim in here is the school swimming pool and sometimes other children even pee inside it," I sulk.

"We didn't have swimming pools in our village at the time. And, it wasn't always fun. Some village folk didn't like girls swimming."

"Why?"

"They used to say 'what sort of girls are these? Not at all lady-like! They are school-going girls and yet run wild'."

"That's silly. Why can't girls swim?"

"Some old people had these bizarre ideas. But not all of them. Others came to our defense. They'd say 'What do you mean 'wild girls'? This girl here can barely swim from shore to shore, but her mother could do several rounds without losing her breath!'"

"Did they listen?"

"Sort of. They would nod sagely and start boasting about the older women in our village and how they could win any competition."

"Did all that bother you Amma?"

"We didn't care what they thought," Amma said with a wink, "Every Saturday and Sunday, we were in the water, from nine in the morning until two in the afternoon".

"What did you even do for that long?"

"Mm…sometimes we set ourselves complicated goals. We'd tie an egg into a towel that we wrapped around our heads. The goal was to swim from one shore to the next without breaking the egg. And sometimes we would stand in line at the river bank and dive in, one after the other, aiming to make as loud a splash as possible. Some adults used to say that they could hear us from miles away!"

"Swimming Sir says that a loud splash means your dive is incorrect."

"Oh psshh! No such thing. Don't you feel like making a huge splash sometimes?" Amma asked.

"YES!!"

"Then the next time we go to the village, I'll take you to the pond where I learnt how to swim and you can dive as many times as you want, make loud splashes, and stay there till your fingertips are wrinkled and you're sick of the water, okay?" Amma suggested.

"Not possible! I love swimming!" I said.

"Me too," Amma smiled and patted my head.

Fussing
Around Insects

AMMA'S INSECT STORIES are the ickiest and most unbelievable of them all. And she won't stop telling them. My feelings on insects are known to everyone at home, and they are: YUCK!

But Amma insists that insects can be beautiful and fantastical and that just because all I see are cockroaches and mosquitoes, I shouldn't think all insects are icky. She often tries telling me about some 'beautiful' insect or the other from her village, and then I wonder if she's just making it up.

"You know, there are so many different kinds of beetles. I saw so many in the village…" she said to me once.

"Eww. I hope they stay there," I replied immediately.

Amma laughed.

"But why are you scared of them? They're harmless if you leave them alone."

"I'm not scared, they're just disgusting and creepy and they crawl everywhere. **Euughhh**," I said, shuddering.

"Some of them do really amazing things."

"Like?"

"Well… there are insects that create chirping sounds by rubbing their legs together…"

"Please, Amma!"

"It's true. How do you think grasshoppers make that sound that you hear every night? They're creating sound from body parts."

"Oh, even I can do that. Mohan taught me how to fart by cupping my hand into my armpit, see like this," I said and showed Amma my new skill.

"See, I'm a grasshopper," I said through the fart sounds, making Amma laugh out really loud.

"At least they're creating music, unlike you," Amma said, poking my arm gently, but still laughing.

"Insects create music?"

"Why, can't they? Have you heard cicadas? They have a distinct humming sound, like the string on an instrument….eeeoooon, eeeeeon, eeeeeeeeon. And that's just one cicada. Imagine what our forests sounded like when a whole chorus starts humming."

I tried imagining it, but the thought of it gave me the creeps.

Amma went on, "My friends and I would actually go looking for cicadas, and when we found one, we would trap it in a matchbox and pretend it was a small radio! And whenever it was season for the king or queen beetle, we would also put them in a box and feed them special 'leaf meals' and watch them lay eggs."

"So insects have seasons, just like fruits?"

"Well, some insects' life cycles depend on the seasons. So, in our village, when it rained in October-November, the forest came alive with insects."

"What kind?"

"Like the fat, red beetle. It looks like a small silky flower on the forest floor. But it's never just the one. They come in the hundreds and thousands. We'd pick them and stuff them into our pockets. And sometimes let them run along our arms and necks, their legs tickling our skin…"

 "Yuck!"

"Then there were the summer insects like dragonflies, which were my favourite. Or the insects that announced the rain."

"How can an insect know when it's going to rain?"

"I don't exactly know how. We just knew that if we saw them, the rainy season would start. And if anyone caught sight of that insect, all the kids would hear of it and we'd hope for really heavy rain so that schools could be shut."

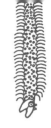

"We're always hoping for rain holidays too," I agreed.

"And then of course, there are the fireflies which are alive for only two months in the whole year."

"Are they those tiny bugs that light up? Torchlight bugs?"

"Yes, they're called fireflies. I loved it when they came, because most of the houses didn't have electricity back then, so when the fireflies sat on a tree outside our house, I would pretend they were street lights. And sometimes, I'd catch a few of them and pretend I was holding a light bulb."

"I want to do that!"

"Oh, not scared of bugs anymore, then?"

"Only the nice ones. All I get to see here are cockroaches."

"You're right; we don't see too many of them here. There were so many in the village! And we wanted to look closely at everything we set our eyes on. We were so intent on catching them that I suppose we ended up tormenting them without really meaning to..." Amma trailed off.

She doesn't like to think back on what they did to the insects. And as much as I dislike insects, I don't either.

During my last summer vacation, when I went to Amma's village, we saw lots of fireflies outside our house. I didn't know what the small dots in the bushes were at first, and yelled for Amma to come to the window quickly. She hurriedly put her face against her glass, squinted for a few seconds, and broke into a smile.

"Fireflies!" she exclaimed.

I couldn't believe it! Actual real-life fireflies! Not just from Amma's stories.

"See?" Amma said, pulling me closer to her, "Didn't I say they were real?

Following
a Peacock

I ONCE ASKED AMMA what her favourite animal was as a child.

"Oh, definitely the peacock!" she said.

"Amma, we see peacocks all the time!"

"Oh, really? When did you see one last?"

"This summer when we went to the zoo for a school picnic!
It looked very tired and bored."

"That's because you saw one in a cage. Have you ever seen one
just a few feet away from you, outside your own house?"

"No...." I replied with suspicion.

"I did. One day, I think it was before the rains, I woke up to
get ready for school and saw a peacock right there, in the field
outside our house! I couldn't believe my eyes and screamed,
"**Aaaaaa... PEACOCK!! A PEACOCK!!!**" and rushed outside, but I then
slowed down so I didn't startle the bird. It had its feathers spread
out like a fan, and it looked so fantastic! I was so excited that
I tried grabbing at it, but it got scared and ran away."

"Oh no!"

Amma nodded, "But it had shed a feather, and I picked it up.
It was so beautiful. I couldn't think of anything else. That year
all I wanted was to have a peacock for a pet. I told everyone that
I wanted a peacock as my reward for not getting into a fight all
week. It's all I could think of."

"You really wanted a peacock for a pet?"

"Okay... to be honest, it's the feathers I wanted. My friends and
I went around looking for baby peacocks, just so we could collect
their feathers. Imagine, we even let boys come with us because
we could always use more help, plus we could wander as far as we
wanted together—sometimes right into the forest. We spent most
of our time in search of very particular peacock feathers..."

"What do you mean? They're all the same"

"If you buy them from the market, yes. But say you were to pick one up yourself, you'd know the difference because they all look different. Some feathers look like knives, some like human eyes, and others look like long swords. Whoever got a hold of a sword feather would yell: 'WATCH OUT! I've got a sword!'"

"And what did they do?"

"I didn't really pay attention to any of that. All I was interested in was in holding a peacock. I wanted to sit on it and have it take me around… but it wasn't easy. They were always very alert and would run away at the least noise. So you had to stay very quiet to catch one."

"Did you try catching one?"

"Oh, I would Crouch for hours waiting."

"Where?"

"In the forest. There was one spot where
they could be found, and I knew it well.
One time I managed to creep up behind
a peacock without it noticing me.
That's the closest I ever got. I could reach
out and touch its feathers—I was that close!
But I knew that I had to move fast because
the peacock wouldn't stand still for long,
so I decided to make a quick grab at
the feathers!"

"And then?" I asked excitedly.

"Of course it shrieked and fluttered
away," Amma said with a sigh, "I ducked and hid
my face, I was scared it would attack me."

"Did it?"

"No…I think we both ended up scaring each other.
But I can still hear its scream and the sound of its feathers
flapping around in panic," Amma paused before continuing.
"And have I told you about when a peacock came to peck at
the grain that our neighbour had spread out to dry in her yard?"

"No."

"Her daughter came running and asked for help. We tried to
get the peacock to move away from the grain but we ended up
shooing the bird right into the neighbour's house!"

"Oh no!!"

"Yes…we didn't know what to do! We panicked and just
locked the door on it."

"So the peacock became your prisoner…"

"Yes, but we suddenly had our first real chance of getting
some feathers."

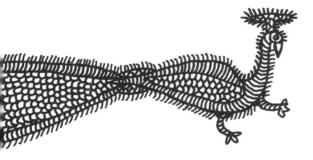

"And did you?"

Amma winked at me, "We did."

"Weren't you scared the peacock would go for you?"

"I think we were just over the moon about getting feathers from
a peacock. And I think it was more scared of us at this point,
than we were of it."

"Once each of us had a few feathers, we slowed down and felt
enough was enough so we let the bird out. It circled the yard
for a bit and flew away."

"That's cruel Amma. Didn't you feel bad about hurting it?"

"At the time, no, we were just thrilled. The feathers—we could
trade them for other things, make stuff with them… but then,
slowly, I started feeling bad. What if someone found out that
we'd picked them off a peacock? We knew we were in for
a scolding. Everyone started feeling bad. We'd tormented that
bird. I felt so guilty that I decided to get rid of the feathers."

"But that wouldn't help the peacock."

"You're right, but as children we thought that if we got rid
of them, we wouldn't need to think of the terrible thing we did."

"So you threw them away?"

"I just gathered them all one day and threw them into the village pond."

I felt strange as Amma told me this.

"But Amma… you're the one who is always telling me to think of how my actions will affect others…"

Amma nodded and softly patted my cheek.

"Yes. How do you think I learnt that lesson?"

AMMA WAS ENTERTAINED by the strangest things as a child. She says that one of her favourite things to do as a kid was to play with her own shadow.

"Didn't it get a bit boring after a while?" I asked.

"Oh, I never tired of playing with my shadow—I loved her. The second I stepped out into the sun or under lamplight, she'd appear. She was always there for me. I'd say, let's run, and she'd run. Stop! And she'd stop. I loved her because she did everything I asked her to."

"Did you ask her to put her books away and do her homework also?"

"Very funny. No, I'd even dance with her. That way I could look at myself dancing even without a mirror. We even played 'Catch' sometimes."

"That's just you running away from your shadow. It's not a real game," I pointed out.

"Well, it depends… if I stepped out of the house and she appeared behind me, I would ask her to catch me."

"And if she appeared in front of you…"

"I would try catching her instead," Amma finished my sentence with a nod before continuing, "I was so curious about her. How did she change shape and position through the day? And how is it that she was shaped like me, but didn't have the clothes that I did? I really wanted to know. I even tried whispering to her when no one was around, just in case she was shy around others."

"Do you remember what you said?"

"I asked her if she was a magician, because I couldn't figure out how she worked and was convinced it had to be magic."

"But didn't you ask anyone else about how shadows worked?"

"No, I was interested in spending more time with her. Whenever there was a big festival, the main roads would be lit up with lanterns. And I'd entertain myself for hours playing with her under the lamplights."

"Did no one think you were weird Amma?"

"Just old people. They'd shake their heads at me and say: 'If you keep looking at your shadow like this, you'll never grow!'"

"But you didn't believe them, right?"

"Actually…the thought of never growing up did worry me. But I couldn't bear to stop playing with her either. So I started looking at her with my eyes half-shut instead."

"Ammaaaaa!"

"What! You never know. Back then, we also believed that shadows turned into ghosts at night."

"That's so silly. There's no such thing as ghosts."

Amma lowered her voice, put her face close to mine and whispered, "Oh yes there are. They are out at all times of the night—you can spot them by their shadows," she said, trying to scare me.

"Ammaaaaa…did you not learn about how shadows work in school? We learnt this in Class 3!"

"I did learn about shadows in school. I forget in which class, but they'd take us to the playground and ask us to stand facing the morning sun. Then, we had to stretch our hands out in front of us and sing this one song…it was really strange… how did it go…"

Amma began to hum:
"On your left is north, on your right, south.
In front of you, east, behind you west,"

"You still remember it!"

"Of course I do. I used to sing the song at home, standing outside our main door, under the morning sun."

"Why?"

"Because someone said that our house was east-facing."

"But what does this have to do with shadows?"

"Nothing, until Uncle Balu came along. I must have been in Class 3 or 4. He found me one morning in front of my house, hitting at my shadow with a stick. He asked me what I was doing, and I told him I was fighting with my shadow friend. He chuckled and said that he knew some secrets about shadows that he could tell me."

"Like what?"

"He asked if I knew that shadows are linked to directions. 'Like east, west, north, south?' I said yes."

"And then he told you the secrets?"

"No, I got a long and boring geography lesson instead."

I groaned in disappointment.

"Anyway, despite Uncle Balu's attempts to ruin my love for shadows, I thought about them all the time. In fact, just a few weeks after he left, someone told me that a shadow puppet theatre would be coming to our village! I was so thrilled—I had never seen a shadow play before!"

"Ooooh!" I said excitedly, "What was it like?"

"We all sat inside a large hut, and there was a white screen in front of us. You could see shadows on it, speaking and moving. But while everyone else was glued to the white screen, I was busy trying to figure out how it all worked. Where did these figures disappear when the light went off behind the screen? Whose shadows were these? And who was singing? Do shadows sing? I was so confused."

"Maybe they were ghosts?"

"Hmm?"

"You only said earlier that shadows without bodies are ghosts."

"Don't be silly. The next day I went to where the shadow puppet people were staying and asked a man where the 'real' people were. But he didn't seem to get what I was asking. So I said to him, but surely there must have been real people behind the screen that created the shadows?"

"And what did he say?"

"He said, 'Oh, but this is shadow play! The whole point is to focus on what is in front of you.' But I still persisted. 'Yes, but where are the real people?' I asked him again. He got a little irritated with me and snapped, saying, 'The real people are not important!'"

Amma laughed and shook her head.

But I didn't get it.

"What did he mean by that, Amma?"

"That I was ignoring the story in front of me to look for something else. And that sometimes, it matters less what the real facts are, but more that the audience enjoys what is being narrated to them."

Ah, I thought. A little bit like Amma's stories.

No?

Mother Plays
with Make-up

AMMA TOLD ME SHE LOVED playing dress-up as a little girl.

"I loved to stand in front of the mirror, put on a sari and powder my face. I use to call it my 'make-up' and would spend hours admiring my reflection."

"Didn't you have proper make-up?"

"No, I only had talcum powder."

"Nothing at all?"

"Nothing. For Diwali, my mother would buy me a set of rubber bangles. And for Pongal, a necklace made of small beads and sometimes, a box of coloured *pottus*. The beads were so flimsy they'd fall off the thread within hours and I had to keep running after them and rescuing the loose ones."

"Why couldn't you just buy another one?"

"Because that's all I would get for the year. If the beads fell apart, I had to collect and thread them on again. But I didn't care for the necklaces that much anyway. It was the pottus I loved. They made me feel very fancy because they came as a powder that you mixed with a bit of oil, not the sticker kind you get now. I loved making designs with them. A line with dots... small dots around a large dot..."

"Like what we do in art class, except on your forehead."

"Yes. But the real fun was with what we could find in the forest."

"More insects and bugs?"

"No. Flowers, leaves, twigs...anything to dress ourselves up."

"How did you do that?"

"Well, certain flowers made perfect nose rings, or...mmm... the leaves of a plant could turn into ornaments."

"Was this just for girls?"

"Of course not. We had boys in our group too. And we all dressed up to act so it didn't matter whether you were a girl or a boy. We'd make crowns out of leaves and stalks and pretend to be kings, or we'd make badges out of flowers and award them to each other, like medals we had won in a great competition."

"You made up your own games?"

"Well sometimes just collecting this stuff was a game—if you want. With the *tazhambu* flower, you've got to be careful though. They grow close to snake-pits."

"Were you ever bitten by a snake?"

"No, thankfully never."

"But why did you want them if picking them was unsafe?"

"Girls would tie tazhambu flowers on their braids using a piece of cardboard."

"And what if someone had short hair?"

"Then you got some false hair, clipped it to your head, and braided it till it reached your waist and then added the tazhambu strip. But, all this stopped when I turned twelve or thirteen."

"But why? Did someone scold you?"

"No, no one scolded me. By then something more exciting happened..."

"What?"

"I started acting."

"What! I don't believe you."

"It's true. I started volunteering to act in village plays whenever they had one. And if I was chosen, I got to put on proper stage make-up."

"Wait, so that's why you stopped dressing up with things from the forest."

Amma nodded.

"What all did you get to do on stage?"

"I loved playing men. It was great fun to wear a turban, or stick on a false mustache. I remember, once I had to play a herdsman and carry a small stick, twirl my mustache and run around the stage singing…"

Amma broke into song:

"The bullock cuts freeeeeee from the cart

And runs with all its MIIIIGHT,

The bull tethered tooooooo its post

runs and is ready for a fi-IIIIIGHT."

"I didn't know you did such fun things when you were young! How come you don't do it anymore?"

"Acting?"

I nodded.

"There weren't that many plays staged in our village. Plus, I never gave up what I loved the most—dressing up to act. We'd watch the plays and then run home to try and recreate them. And because we didn't have too much money, we even made our own make-up kit from all sorts of stuff."

"Like?"

"Let's see... face paint from powder mixed with water; mustaches with *mai*; *kumkumam* for pink cheeks..."

"I used sketch-pens on my face and shirt to dress-up too!" I said excitedly.

"Yes, you did! I remember struggling to wash your uniform," Amma chuckled, and hurried to answer the doorbell.

I tried to imagine Amma as a young girl drawing on a big curly mustache and applying kumkumam on her cheeks. But... I think she enjoyed acting more than the make-up.

I wonder sometimes if (like me) Amma also secretly pretends to be a superhero.

Mother Loves
the Dark

AMMA IS FOND OF THE DARK, and I find that really strange. I love sunlight and bright things, so I'm always on the hunt for famous quotes on darkness and evil to use in my arguments with her.

"What is done in the dark will come to light," I told her one day, after reading it in our Moral Science textbook.

"Then stop doing things in the dark," Amma retorted.

I then tried singing a song from our school assembly over dinner between mouthfuls of rice. The song was about how children are the light of the world and I thought it was a great example but Amma shook her head.

"Not the same thing," she shook her head.

"See, if you were used to the darkness as a child like I was, you would learn to be fond of it," she explained.

"What do you mean?"

"For me, the dark always meant story-time, and that meant sitting close to grandmother as she told me stories of sinister magicians who walked the ocean floor. Plus my friends and I used to love nightfall because we had games that we played only at night. And sometimes—I think on the full moon nights—adults joined in."

"You really played all night?"

"Well… we wanted to… but night time was also for watching all the interesting people who worked in the dark—rabbit hunters, night fishermen, water supervisors…"

"Water supervisors?"

"They had to keep watch and make sure that no field in the village got more than its share of water. In my head, all of these people were like the brave heroes from grandmother's stories, venturing into the night to fight the sinister magicians. I would beg them to tell me about their adventures but they always pretended to be in a hurry. But actually, they loved to sit and share stories."

"Just like you," I wanted to say, but knew better and decided to cough instead.

"Of course, the dark is not only for stories or play..."

"It's for sleep and rest too!" I chimed in.

"For most humans, yes, but many plants and animals need the darkness to carry out important tasks. It's just that you and I aren't awake to watch what happens."

"So, how did you know?" I asked.

"Because we played so much in the dark back then. We saw dogs and scorpions and centipedes and snakes and cicadas go about freely... even ghosts."

"As IF!" I exclaimed.

"What? It's true! Grandmother used to tell me so many creepy stories about the dark. All the evil magicians in her stories come out only when it's pitch black. I used to beg her to tell me a story every night just before bedtime. Sometimes, I'd fall asleep right in the middle of a story. But somehow the story continued in my dreams.

"My Amma—your grandmother—was a light sleeper. She'd wake up at the slightest sound. Actually, her ears would tingle awake first, so she heard things before she saw them. Like the time she heard the big black scorpion that crept into my bed. I didn't hear it because I was fast asleep, but she heard it just as it was about to graze my leg and pulled me away."

I looked at Amma in disbelief. Did my grandmother really have ears like antennae that alerted her to approaching creepy crawlies?

"Oh! Did I tell you about the time one of our neighbours discovered hyenas in the forest next to their field?" Amma suddenly asked.

I shook my head vigorously.

"So… they had heard a strange noise in the dead of the night. eee-eee-EEEEEE! eee-eeeeee-EEEEE! When they went to look, they stumbled near a group of hyenas skulking around the field at the back of their house!"

"Really?? Was that the first time you all saw hyenas?"

"Yes, but it wasn't the last time. For almost a whole month after that, we saw those hyenas every night. I just had to think of a hyena and it would appear out of nowhere..."

"That must be scary...the only animals that come out at night are dangerous ones," I said.

"My friends and I were no less dangerous," Amma chuckles, "always ready to slip out of the house for the slightest reason."

"How did you even see anything in the dark?"

"We had to learn to do it."

"How?"

"Well...think about it, at first you can't really see your way ahead, no? Every step feels dangerous. And if you hear strange animal noises in the distance, it's even creepier. But once you spend some time in the dark, your eyes become used to it and you could roam around the village without difficulty."

"I wouldn't want to play a game like that in the night," I shuddered, "You can't tell what will happen."

"Which is the best part...it can be so much fun! Look up at the sky and spot the moon for a second, look up again and it's gone! By the time I'd yell to my friends about the moon being kidnapped, the clouds would be gone, and you could see the moon again."

"You really weren't scared of the dark?" I asked, still not convinced.

"Not really, I always thought of it as an adventure. On nights that we had nothing else to do, my friends and I would take leftover food from our homes and save them to eat at midnight. There's something about eating food when you're not otherwise supposed to..."

"You never let **ME** eat at midnight," I grumbled, but it was unclear if Amma had heard me.

If I had my way, I would also listen to stories, eat all the food I wanted and play with my friends outside and never sleep!

But then... I think of the wild animals, strange sounds, and creepy crawlies in the dark. Hmm... maybe not. I'm not as brave as Amma yet.

MOTHER STEALS A BICYCLE AND OTHER STORIES
Based on Salai Selvam's original Tamil text
and translated into English by V. Geetha

Copyright ©2018 Tara Books Pvt. Ltd.

For the text: Salai Selvam, Shruti Buddhavarapu
For the illustrations: Tejubehan
Design: Dhwani Shah

For this edition:
Tara Books Pvt. Ltd., India, tarabooks.com
and Tara Publishing Ltd., tarabooks.com/uk

Production: C. Arumugam

Printed in India by Canara Traders and Printers

Versions of these stories have appeared
previously in *Hindu Tamizh Thisai*

ISBN: 978-81-934485-1-9